# Camilla Chameleon

For Jasmine and Raven — C.S.

To my big sister, Marie, who never
disappeared when I needed her — P.C.

Text © 2005 Colleen Sydor
Illustrations © 2005 Pascale Constantin

Kids Can Press acknowledges the financial support of the Government of Ontario,
through the Ontario Media Development Corporation's Ontario Book Initiative; the
Ontario Arts Council; the Canada Council for the Arts; and the Government of Canada,
through the BPIDP, for our publishing activity.

Published in Canada by
Kids Can Press Ltd.
29 Birch Avenue
Toronto, ON  M4V 1E2

Published in the U.S. by
Kids Can Press Ltd.
2250 Military Road
Tonawanda, NY  14150

www.kidscanpress.com

The artwork in this book was rendered in oil.
The text is set in Souvenir.

Edited by Tara Walker
Designed by Karen Powers
Printed and bound in China

This book is smyth sewn casebound.

CM 05  0 9 8 7 6 5 4 3 2 1

**Library and Archives Canada Cataloguing in Publication**

Sydor, Colleen
    Camilla chameleon / written by Colleen Sydor ;
illustrated by Pascale Constantin.

ISBN 1-55337-482-7

I. Constantin, Pascale  II. Title.

PS8587.Y36C34 2005    jC813'.54    C2004-906570-X

Kids Can Press is a *Corus*™ Entertainment company

# Camilla Chameleon

Written by Colleen Sydor

Illustrated by Pascale Constantin

KIDS CAN PRESS

One day Willy McNilly came home from work to find the kitchen littered with empty cans of Cream of Chameleon soup. Upstairs he found his wife still in bed, surrounded by mountains of empty soup bowls.

"What can I get you for supper, my dear?" asked Mr. McNilly.

"Some Cream of Chameleon soup, please," was his wife's reply. And from that day on it was Cream of Chameleon soup for breakfast, Cream of Chameleon soup for lunch and Cream of Chameleon soup for supper.

Mr. McNilly began to worry. Especially when he noticed his wife looking more and more like she'd swallowed a beachball. The morning she complained of a tummy ache, he put on his hat. "That's it, Milly!" he said. "I'm taking you to see Dr. Proctor."

Dr. Proctor examined Mrs. McNilly. He looked at Mr. McNilly gravely. He looked at Mrs. McNilly grimly. Then he broke out into a great big grin. "Congratulations, Willy and Milly. You're going to have a baby!"

The McNillys were delighted when Camilla came into the world —
a healthy bouncing baby girl. She *was* a little
strange looking, but her parents thought
she was perfect!

Mr. and Mrs. McNilly could barely keep their eyes off their new daughter. The one time they *did* look away (just long enough for a quick game of Crazy Eights), Camilla seemed to disappear into thin air. The McNillys had a dilly of a time finding her.

"Check inside the bread box," said Mr. McNilly.

"I did!" said Mrs. McNilly. "Have a look in the umbrella stand."

"Odd," said Mr. McNilly when he finally found Camilla right where he'd left her. "I could have sworn this shoe box was empty a minute ago."

As she got older (and wiser) Camilla learned to camouflage herself at just the right times — twice a year at Dr. Proctor's office, frequently when Auntie Dicky came to visit and, dependably, every Saturday night at six o'clock. (On Saturday nights Mrs. McNilly served Mr. McNilly's favorite supper: liver and onions with fried cabbage.)

At school Camilla was the most popular kid in her class. The other children were awed by her incredible hide-and-seek abilities. They were impressed with how she could pick up a hopscotch rock without even bending over.

They admired how she could look straight at Miss Floxbottom with one eye and read a comic book with the other. But what puzzled her classmates was how Camilla seemed to be absent every time Miss Floxbottom asked for a volunteer to clean the hamster cage.

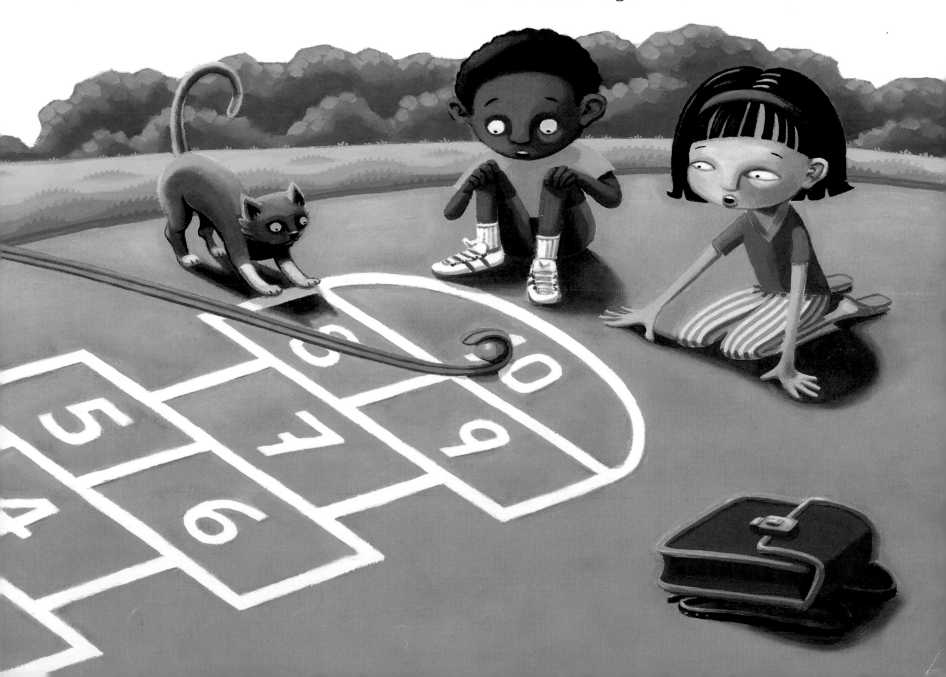

"Class," said Miss Floxbottom one day,
"I need someone to write the homework
answers on the blackboard."

While her classmates slipped down in
their seats, Camilla continued reading her
comic book.

*"Camilla!"* said Miss Floxbottom.
"I think it's *your* turn to volunteer."

Camilla looked down at her blank
page. Instead of doing homework the
night before, she'd watched the Monday
night movie with her parents. (Of course,
Mr. and Mrs. McNilly had no idea they
were watching the movie with their
daughter. Although they *did* wonder how
the popcorn disappeared so fast.)

Camilla walked to the front
of the room. She waited until her
teacher distracted the class with a
tricky subtraction question. Then she
blended into the blackboard.

When Miss Floxbottom turned
around, Camilla was nowhere to be seen.

Miss Floxbottom looked inside the
broom closet. She peeked underneath
her big oak desk. She stepped out the
door and peered down the hall.

"Where in the world is Camilla
McNilly?" demanded Miss Floxbottom.

The room fell silent. No one moved a muscle (unless you count twenty-six sets of eyeballs looking in twenty-six different directions for Camilla).

"Well, well, well," said Miss Floxbottom, spying a can of Fizzy Fizzy Make Ya Dizzy Rootin' Tootin' Root Beer on the chalk ledge. Everyone knew there was only one kid in the class whose mother allowed her to bring Fizzy Fizzy Make Ya Dizzy Rootin' Tootin' Root Beer for lunch — the very same kid who was presently causing the blackboard to blink.

"I will repeat my question," said Miss Floxbottom. "*Where* is Miss McNilly?"

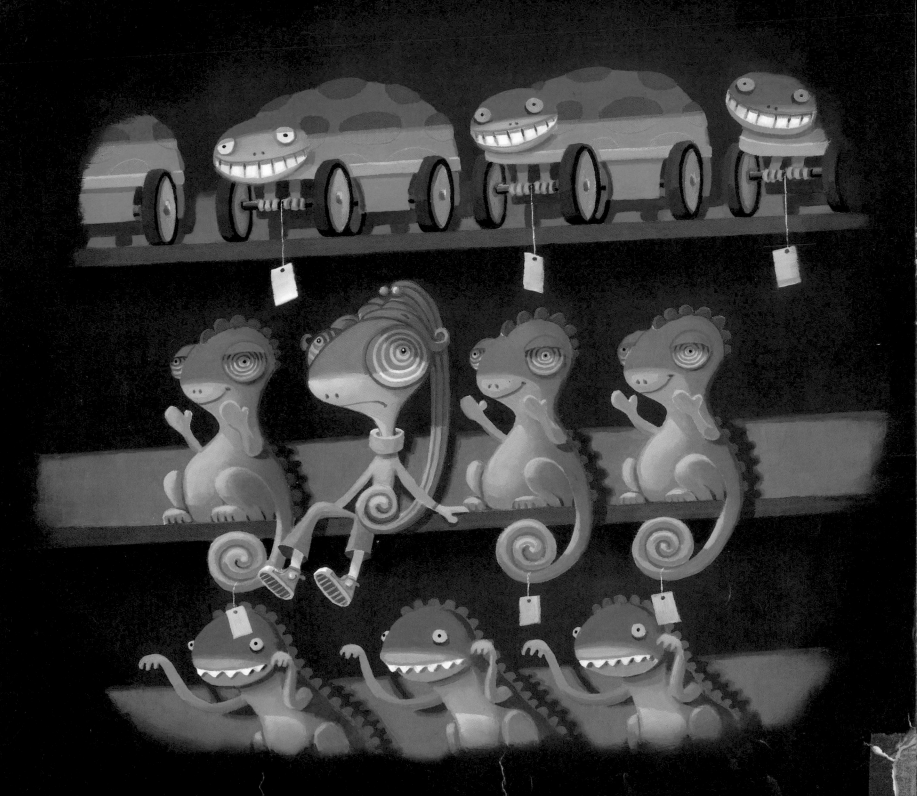

At first Camilla wasn't the least bit worried. She was perfectly camouflaged. And she'd been in far worse jams. Like the time she'd blended into the toy section at FardsMart Superstore and got locked in for the night. But today Camilla had no idea what she was getting herself into. Just minutes before, she'd bolted down not one, but *two* cans of Fizzy Fizzy Make Ya Dizzy Rootin' Tootin' Root Beer, and now she felt a rumble in her tummy.

*Uh-oh*, thought Camilla. She knew what that meant. It was the Rootin' Tootin' carbonated bubbles begging to come up, and they weren't taking no for an answer.

Camilla tried to hold them back
(she really did), but in the end she couldn't.
Suddenly her mouth blew open and out ripped
a belch so tremendous it shook the entire room.

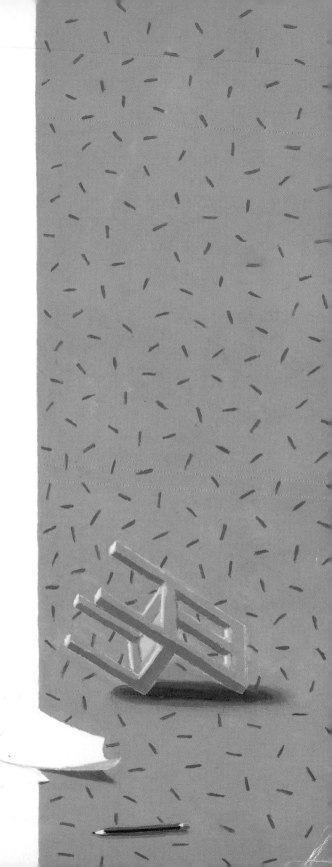

Miss Floxbottom jumped. Her jaw dropped. She spun around, and who did she see slowly appearing before her very eyes? Camilla McNilly, light pink at first, darkening to bright red from head to toe. Camilla was mortified. Her classmates were flabbergasted (although delighted to add "power-belching" to Camilla's long list of talents).

Miss Floxbottom sighed and shook her head. She'd once had a silly goose as a student and, over the years, plenty of lazy sloths, but never a clever chameleon. Hold on, thought Miss Floxbottom, a *chameleon* …

"Camilla!" she boomed. "Come with me."

Miss Floxbottom marched Camilla out of the class, down the hall, past the principal's office (whew!) and straight into the drama room, closing the door behind them.

When she got home from school that day, Camilla bumped
into her father. He was on his way to FardsMart for a crate of
Cream of Pterodactyl soup to satisfy his dear wife's latest craving.
"Wanna come?" he asked.

"Can't, Daddy-o," said Camilla. "I've got tons of homework." She didn't bother telling her father why Miss Floxbottom had assigned her an extra hundred pages of memorization.

Having Camilla in the drama club was a dream come true for Miss Floxbottom. She had always wished for an invisible helper to whisper forgotten lines into the ears of dumbstruck actors. With Camilla's expert help, the next school play was as smooth as Funky-No-Chunky Smoothy-Woothy Peanut Butter.

At the end of the play Camilla appeared on stage with the rest of the cast. Her parents gave her a Silly-McNilly standing ovation. (They never did figure out which part Camilla played, but they *knew* her acting must have been splendid.) Miss Floxbottom even led a special round of applause for Camilla, who was tickled pink. Camilla realized that as talented as she was at blending in, she liked standing out even better!

Not long afterwards Camilla became a big sister. Her mother gave birth to a bouncing baby boy named Terry. Even though he had a face like a pterodactyl, Mr. and Mrs. McNilly thought he was perfect!

On the day that Camilla discovered Terry could fly, she took him aside.

"Terry," she said, "we're performing *Peter Pan* for the school play this year, and I think you'd make a perfect Tinker Bell. Don't worry — I'll help you with your lines. And, Terry?" she added. "The day Mom starts craving Cream of Alligator soup is the day we pack our bags. Deal?"

"Deal," said Terry.

Actually, Al turned out to be a rather sweet baby
brother, even though he *was* a little strange looking!